Angel of the Harbor

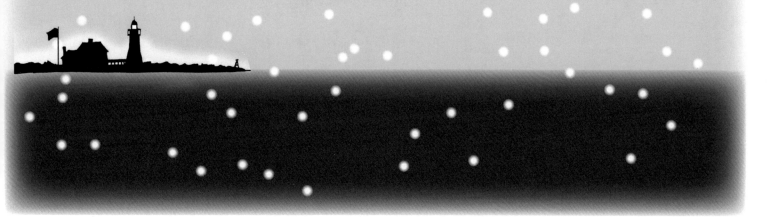

Written by Chris Toto Zaremba • Illustrated by Susan S. Petersen

Happy Holidays!
~Chris Z

Have fun
Sue Petersen

Written and Published by Chris Toto Zaremba
Scituate, Massachusetts
ctzaremba@gmail.com

Illustrations/Design by Susan S. Petersen
Hanover, Massachusetts
Sue@sspetersen.com

Printed in the United States of America

ISBN 978-1539312918

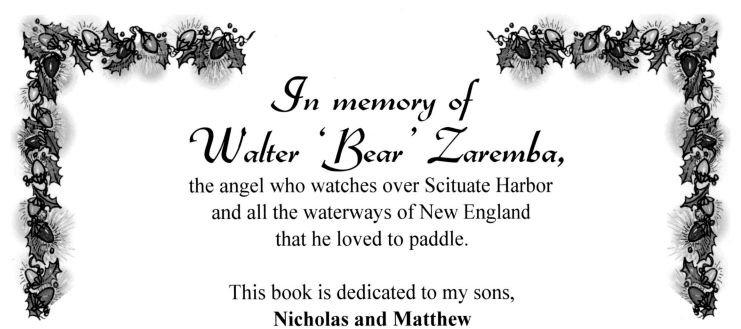

In memory of
Walter 'Bear' Zaremba,
the angel who watches over Scituate Harbor
and all the waterways of New England
that he loved to paddle.

This book is dedicated to my sons,
Nicholas and Matthew
whose creativity encouraged me
to rediscover and embrace my own.

Special thanks to Sue
whose illustrations helped bring my poem to life.

May everyone who reads this book
be reminded to believe in
all the wondrous things out there in the universe
like angels, love, and the great unknown!

Peace and Merry Christmas,
Chris

T'was three weeks before Christmas and all through the town
white lights were hanging, there was snow on the ground.
The children let out from their schools everywhere
and rushed to the harbor for the big winter fair.

3.

The mood it was merry,
their cheeks, they were cherry,
as they waited for Santa's big ferry.

4.

Every shop was decked out with wreaths green and bows red.
Every person wore mittens, a scarf, and a hat on their head.

5.

6.

Hot chocolate with marshmallows
or whipped cream piled on top
was the choice of the children
which no one dared stop.

The Harbor Master seemed concerned
as he searched in his boat.

9.

The wind chimes began to
sing with the breeze.
I looked down the beach,
I looked at the sea.

The buoys danced with a cling
and then a clang.
The waves breached the wall
while the choir still sang.

But the cold was too much with more snow then some sleet.
Parents gathered the children and emptied Front Street.

"This won't do!", cried a woman. (Santa's wife we did think) as she stood on the pier, with hair white and face pink.

13.

An angel on high knew something must be done
or a wonderful night would no longer be fun.

So he reached for the moon to quiet the tide.
The waves settled down for a soft winter's ride.

14

He moved the clouds so the stars filled the sky.
The people looked up and exclaimed, "Oh my, my!"
As they stood watching the magic
of Northern Lights, blue and green,
they heard reindeer bells,
but Santa could not be seen.

Though they all heard a message
as the bells faded away:
"I'll be back to visit,
the eve of Christmas Day.

Send me your letters.
there are cookies to bake.
And be good girls and boys,
for goodness sake."

Everyone was so happy,
they wished each other good night
as they headed for home
by the full moon's light.

Days passed on by as Christmas drew near.

The letters got mailed.
Santa soon will be here.

19.

For years later the people remembered that storm.
It was one of those nights, it was out of the norm.

20.

Something happened that night, everyone knew.
The Spirit of Christmas came to me and to you...

21.

Made in the USA
Middletown, DE
30 October 2016